The Right Kind of Friend

Eleanor Robins

High Noon Books
Novato, California

Cover Design: Jill Zwicky
Interior Illustrations: Rick Hackney

International Standard Book Number: 1-57128-180-0

9 8 7 6 5 4 3 2 1 0
0 9 8 7 6 5 4 3 2 1

Contents

CHAPTER 1

The New Girl

Jen was on her way to school. Her best friend Fran was with her. They lived on the same block near the school.

"Walk faster, Jen. We need to hurry," Fran said.

"Why? We won't be late," Jen said.

"I have to copy your math," Fran said.

Fran had copied Jen's math homework four times in the last two weeks.

"Why didn't you do it?" Jen asked.

"I wanted to do something else," Fran said.

"You need to do your homework. Or you won't know how to do the math," Jen said.

"Keep doing your homework right, and I'll be OK. Now walk faster," Fran said.

Jen walked faster.

Soon they were at school.

"We have to go right to our homeroom. I need to copy your homework now," Fran said.

"I have to go to my locker first. I want to get my science book," Jen said.

"That can wait," Fran said.

Jen said, "I have to get it now. I might not have time after homeroom."

"OK. But hurry," Fran said.

Fran didn't look pleased.

Jen tried to hurry. She didn't look where she was walking. She bumped into a girl. The girl's books fell on the floor.

"Sorry, I didn't mean to do that," Jen said.

"That's OK. I was looking for a classroom. My homeroom class is in there today. I've been here only three weeks. I still can't find my way around," the girl said.

She told Jen what room she was looking for. And Jen told her where it was. Then Jen helped her pick up her books.

"Next time tell a friend. I'm sure she would help you find the classroom," Jen said.

"I haven't made any friends. It's hard to be a

new girl at school. Most girls have made their friends by now. And they aren't looking for new ones," the girl said.

Jen was new last year. It had been that way for her, too.

Jen knew she had to go. Fran would wonder where she was. She quickly got her science book. She hurried to her homeroom.

"It's about time you got here. Give me your homework," Fran snapped at her.

At times Jen wondered why she wanted to stay friends with Fran. But last year had been a bad time for Jen. Then Fran had wanted to be her friend. Jen didn't have to be by herself any more.

Fran always liked to have her way. At times

she wasn't nice to people. But maybe all friends were like that.

School was over for the day before Jen saw Fran again.

Jen said, "Do you want to go to the track and run? Track practice starts next week."

She and Fran had both been on the track team last year. They were both planning to go out for track this year.

"Track practice hasn't started yet. So I don't want to run. We'll be doing enough of that when practice starts," Fran said.

Jen didn't go to the track to run. She walked home with Fran.

Jen didn't like to do things by herself.

CHAPTER 2

PE Class

It was the next morning. Jen was in her PE class. Fran was in her class, too.

Coach Lane was their teacher. She was also the track coach for the girls.

Coach Lane said, "We are going to race with Coach Clark's class."

Coach Clark was the track coach for the boys.

The class yelled. It was the first time they had raced with his class.

Coach Lane said, "The boys in both classes will race with Coach Clark. The girls from both classes will race with me."

Fran looked at Jen. She said, "This will be fun. I can beat the boys in our class and the boys in Coach Clark's class, too."

The class ran outside. They saw Coach Clark's class. They were next to the track.

Jen's class ran to the track. The boys from Jen's class went over to Coach Clark. His girls came over to Coach Lane. Then all the boys went to the other side of the track.

Coach Lane said, "The girls from Coach Clark's class get in one line. My girls get in a line next to them. You will race two at a time. I'll time the winner."

The girls made two lines.

Jen looked over at Coach Clark's girls. She counted to see who would race with her. It was the girl she had run into the day before.

The girl looked over at Jen. She smiled and waved. Jen smiled and waved back.

"Who is that? I've never seen her before," Fran said.

"She's new. I don't know her name," Jen said.

Soon it was time for Jen and the girl to race. Jen ran as fast as she could. But the girl beat her.

Coach Lane looked down at her watch. She said, "Great time."

Jen ran as fast as she could.
But the new girl beat her.

"Thanks," the girl said.

"What's your name?" Coach Lane asked.

"Kit," the girl said.

"I have never seen you run before. You should go out for track this year," Coach Lane said.

"I don't know. I have never run on a school team," Kit said.

"Think about it," Coach Lane said.

"I can beat that girl. And it won't be hard at all," Fran said to Jen.

Fran was the fastest girl runner in Coach Lane's class.

Soon Fran got to race with Kit. Kit won. Fran looked mad.

Coach Lane said, "Great time again, Kit. You must go out for the track team. We sure could use you on our short relay team."

"I don't know how to run in a relay," Kit said.

"That's OK. You can learn how. We start practice next week," Coach Lane said.

Jen had been on the relay team last year. And so had Fran. She wanted to be on it again this year.

All the girls from last year would be back. There wasn't a place on the relay team for a new girl.

CHAPTER 3

Give Me Your Paper

School was over for the day. Jen met Fran in front of the school.

A girl bumped into Fran. She hadn't meant to do it.

Fran yelled at her. "Watch what you're doing. What's wrong with you?"

"Sorry," the girl said. She hurried off.

"You didn't have to yell at her, Fran. She didn't mean to do it," Jen said.

"She should watch where she's going," Fran

said. She was frowning.

The girls started to walk home.

"PE was fun today. I hope we can race with Coach Clark's class again," Jen said.

"I didn't think it was fun. That new girl had to show off," Fran said.

"I didn't think she was showing off. She just runs fast. Do you think she will go out for track?" Jen asked.

"I hope not. She shouldn't be on the team. She wasn't here last year," Fran said.

"That doesn't matter, I was new last year, too," Jen said.

Fran said, "It's not the same. You better hope she doesn't go out for the team."

"Why?" Jen asked.

"Don't you know what will happen?" Fran asked.

"No. What?" Jen asked.

"She'll take your place on the relay team. And then you won't be on it. I run faster than you do. So she won't take my place," Fran said.

Jen had not thought about that. But fair was fair. The faster girl should be on the team. Of course, Jen still wanted to be on it.

Soon the girls were at Jen's house.

"See you in the morning," Fran said.

"Don't forget to do your math homework. You have to do it by yourself. Miss Miles said we couldn't get any help on it," Jen said.

"I can't worry about that now. I have things to do," Fran said. But she didn't tell Jen what it was she had to do.

Jen had a lot of homework that night. She went to her room and started on it.

The next morning Jen's doorbell rang. Jen went to the door. She looked through the peephole to see who was there. Then she opened the door.

"Fran, why are you here now? It isn't time to go to school yet," Jen said.

"I need to copy your homework. I can't do it at school. Someone might see me," Fran said.

"I can't let you copy today. Don't you remember? Miss Miles said we had to do our own work," Jen said.

"Well, I didn't. So I need to copy yours. No one will know," Fran said.

"But we'll know." Jen said.

"Are we friends?" Fran asked.

"You know we are," Jen said.

"Then give me your paper. We don't want to be late to school," Fran said.

Jen felt bad about it. But she let Fran copy her paper.

CHAPTER 4

Did She Copy?

It was time for math class. Miss Miles took up their homework before class started. They never knew when she would do that.

"I'm going to grade your papers now. I need to see how you did on your homework. Then I can help you with what you did wrong," Miss Miles said.

She gave them work to do in their books. Then she graded the papers. After that she helped them with what they missed.

Most of the time Jen did well in math. But she had missed a lot on her homework. She had thought she knew how to do it. But she had been wrong.

It was time for class to be over.

Miss Miles said, "Jen and Fran, I need to see you after lunch. I'll meet you here when lunch is over."

Jen started to feel very bad. She and Fran had all the same wrong answers. She knew that must be why Miss Miles wanted to talk to them.

Jen said, "She knows one of us copied."

"Don't worry. She just thinks one of us did. She doesn't know which one," Fran said.

"She might ask me. Then I'll have to tell her

you copied. I can't lie to a teacher," Jen said.

"Sure you can," Fran said.

"No, I can't," Jen said.

"OK. OK. So don't get so upset. You don't have to lie."

"Good. Then you'll tell her yourself," Jen said.

"You must be kidding, Jen. No way would I do that," Fran said.

"You know she'll ask me," Jen said.

Fran said, "Don't say a word. Let me do all the talking."

"But I'm sure she will ask me," Jen said. She knew she couldn't lie. She wasn't like that.

Fran said, "OK. Here is what you do. Tell

her I don't need to copy. That I'm able to do my own work. Is that a lie?"

"No," Jen said. It was true. Fran was smart. Fran just didn't like to do her work.

Jen didn't eat much of her lunch. She was too worried.

It was time to see Miss Miles. The girls went into her room.

Miss Miles was sitting at her desk.

"We're here. Just like you told us to be. Why did you want to see us?" Fran said.

"I think you know," Miss Miles said.

"No, we don't, Miss Miles," Fran said.

Jen didn't say anything.

Miss Miles picked up two papers from her

"Why did you want to see us?"

desk. "One of these papers is yours, Fran. The other is yours, Jen."

"Yes, they are," Fran said.

"You both have the same answers. You both did the math wrong. And you did it wrong the same way," Miss Miles said.

"What do you mean, Miss Miles?" Fran asked.

"I think one of you copied," Miss Miles said.

"You are wrong, Miss Miles. I did my own work. And Jen did her own work," Fran said.

Jen didn't say anything.

"Is that right, Jen?" Miss Miles said.

Jen still didn't say anything.

"Did you copy Fran's work?" Miss Miles

asked Jen.

"No," Jen said.

"Did Fran copy your paper?" Miss Miles asked Jen.

At first Jen didn't say anything. She didn't want to lie. But Fran was her friend. She didn't want to get Fran in trouble.

Jen thought about what Fran had told her to say. She said, "Fran doesn't have to copy. She's able to do her own work."

"I know you don't lie, Jen. So I'm sorry I thought one of you had copied." Miss Miles said.

Fran said, "Is that all? May we go now?"

"Yes," Miss Miles said.

Jen and Fran left quickly.

23

They hurried away from the classroom.

Fran said, "I said you wouldn't have to lie. And you didn't. See? I was right."

Jen didn't feel good about herself. She hadn't really lied. But she sure felt like she had.

Fran didn't seem to feel bad at all.

CHAPTER 5

At the Track

School was over for the day. Jen was still upset. She went to her locker to get her track shoes.

She met Fran in front of the school.

"I'm going to the track and run. Do you want to come?" Jen asked Fran.

"I told you the other day. Track practice hasn't started yet. I'll wait until then to run," Fran said.

"OK. See you later," Jen said.

Fran didn't look pleased.

Jen ran down to the track. Some girls were there. Some boys were, too.

She saw Kit. Kit saw her and waved. She jogged over to Jen.

"Hi. Are you going to run?" she asked.

"Yes," Jen said.

"I haven't seen you down here at the track after school before," Kit said.

"Most of the time I run near my house. But I wanted to get used to running on the track. Do you run here every day?" Jen asked.

"When I can. I like to run. It makes me feel good," Kit said.

It made Jen feel good, too.

The girls started to run. They ran slowly so they could talk.

"Are you going out for the track team?" Jen asked.

Kit said, "I don't know. I want to. But I'm not sure what to do."

"Why?" Jen asked.

At first Kit didn't say anything. Jen thought Kit wasn't going to answer.

Then Kit said, "I'm afraid I won't be as good as the other girls. Then I won't make the team."

"I'm sure you will. You run very fast," Jen told her.

The girls ran for a few more minutes.

Then Kit said, "The coach said something

about a relay team. I don't know how to run in a relay."

"You can learn. I'll help you," Jen said.

"Then maybe I will go out for the team. Thanks," Kit said.

Jen didn't think Fran had ever thanked her for anything.

CHAPTER 6

The Relay Team

It was the next week. Jen and Fran were at track practice. Kit was there, too.

Coach Lane walked over to Jen and Fran. She had a baton in her hand.

Gail and Peg were with her. They had been on the relay team last year. Kit was with her, too.

Coach Lane said, "I want you to work on the relay now. Next week I will pick the four girls for the team. The other girl will be the backup runner."

Jen knew she was the slowest runner. She was sure she would be the backup runner.

Then Coach Lane showed Kit how to hold the baton. She said, "You have to run fast. But you must have good teamwork to win."

Two girls called to Coach Lane. "I need to see what they want. Fran and Jen, you tell Kit a little about running a relay. I'll be back in a few minutes," Coach Lane said.

Coach Lane gave the baton to Jen. Then she left to talk to the two girls who had called her.

Jen said, "We run a short relay. So you have to keep the baton in the same hand. You can't move it to the other hand."

Fran said, "You have to pass the baton to a

*Coach Lane showed Kit
how to hold the baton.*

teammate. That's the hard part. Most runners can't do that well. That's why it isn't easy to make the relay team."

Jen said, "You don't look at the runner with the baton. You put your hand back. And the runner will give you the baton."

Jen and Fran showed Kit how they passed the baton.

"See. It isn't easy. It takes a lot of practice," Fran said.

"How do you know when the baton will be passed to you?" Kit asked.

Jen said, "We have a word we yell when we pass. The word is 'NOW.' When we hear that word, we know we will get the baton."

Coach Lane walked back over to them.

"I was watching you pass, girls. You did a good job," Coach Lane said.

Fran didn't say anything. She just stood there.

Coach Lane handed the baton to Gail. She said, "Gail, you started the team off last year. You did a good job. So I want you to be the first runner."

Gail walked over to the starting block.

"All of you work a lot on your passing. You must pass well to win. Make a bad pass, and the race may be lost," Coach Lane said.

Jen worked very hard on her passing during the practice. She hoped she was doing better.

CHAPTER 7

The Baton Is Dropped

It was the next week. Jen was at practice. She was with Fran.

"I'm sure Kit will make the team. And not me," Jen said.

"I know she's faster. But you know how to pass the baton well. She doesn't," Fran said.

"We can stay after practice and work with her. Then she'll get better," Jen said.

"I don't want to work with her. I want you on the team. Not her," Fran said.

Jen wanted to be on the team. But the best runner should be on the team. And that was Kit.

The girls worked very hard. Soon practice was over for the day.

Kit came over to Jen. She said, "I need more help on how to pass. Can you stay and help me?"

"Sure. For a little while," Jen said.

"You can't, you need to do something with me. You can help her tomorrow," Fran said.

"I told Kit I would stay today," Jen said.

Fran said, "I'll stay tomorrow and help, too."

Jen was surprised that Fran said she would help Kit.

"Is that OK?" Jen asked Kit.

"Sure. I'll see you tomorrow," Kit said.

Jen and Fran started to walk home. "What do I need to do with you?" she asked Fran.

Fran said, "Sorry, I forgot. It's next week that I need your help. It's not today."

Kit had left school when Jen and Fran did. It was too late to go back and help her.

The next afternoon, Jen was at track practice. She was with the girls on the relay team.

Coach Lane came over to them.

Fran said, "When will you name the starting four?"

"At the end of practice tomorrow. Work hard. I'll be over to watch you later," Coach Lane said.

The girls worked hard. At times Jen gave the

baton to Kit. At times Fran gave it to Kit. Then they gave the baton to one another.

Coach Lane came over to watch. She told Jen to watch, too. The other four girls would run the relay.

Gail ran first. She gave the baton to Peg.

Peg ran and gave the baton to Fran.

Fran ran with the baton. Then it was time for Fran to give the baton to Kit. Kit dropped the baton.

Coach Lane said, "That's all for today. See you tomorrow."

Kit went over to Fran. She looked upset. Jen couldn't hear what she said to Fran.

But she could hear Fran.

"Don't blame me. I didn't make you drop the baton," Fran yelled at Kit.

Kit ran off. Jen didn't get to talk to her.

Jen wished she had stayed late and helped Kit the day before.

CHAPTER 8

The Right Kind of Friend

Jen looked for Kit at school the next day. But she didn't see her until track practice.

Jen went over to Kit. She said, "I'm sorry about what happened. And I'm sorry I didn't stay and help you."

"It's not your fault," Kit said.

"I should have practiced with you. Then maybe you wouldn't have dropped the baton. I'll stay and help you today," Jen said.

At first Kit didn't say anything. She said,

"Don't blame yourself. Fran wanted me to drop the baton. She planned it that way."

"What do you mean?" Jen said.

"She said *now*. But she waited to pass me the baton," Kit said.

"Fran is my friend. I don't think she would do that. You must be wrong," Jen said.

"Think what you want to. She's your friend. But I know she did it," Kit said.

Coach Lane called the relay team over to her.

Coach Lane said, "I saw that Fran and Kit don't seem to work well together. Jen, you run today."

Fran looked very pleased.

Then Coach Lane said, "Fran, you watch."

40

Fran looked mad. She said, "I'm not the one who dropped the baton."

Coach Lane said, "I know you didn't, Fran. I was watching. But sometimes you don't work well as part of a team."

Fran called Jen over to her. She looked very mad.

"I thought I got Kit off the team. But I didn't. So today you make her drop the baton. Then we'll get her off the team for sure," Fran said.

"No, I won't," Jen said.

Jen couldn't believe Fran thought she would do it. What kind of person did Fran think she was?

"Are we friends?" Fran asked.

"You know we are," Jen said. But now she wasn't sure she wanted to be Fran's friend.

"Then you'll make Kit drop the baton," Fran said.

"I won't do that," Jen said. The right kind of friend wouldn't ask her to do that.

"Then you won't be my friend," Fran said. She still looked very mad.

Jen thought about her friendship with Fran. Jen had let Fran copy her homework. She had not told the truth to Miss Miles about their work. And now Fran wanted her to help get Kit off the track team.

Fran seemed to bring out the worst in her.

Jen needed a friend who would bring out the best in her.

"Well, are you going to do it or not?" Fran said.

"I told you. No," Jen said.

"Then you won't be my friend any longer. What do you say now?" Fran said.

"That's fine with me, Fran," Jen said.

Fran looked very surprised. She looked at Jen. She didn't seem to know what to say.

Jen said, "You seem to bring out the worst in me. I don't need a friend like that. I need a friend who brings out the best in me."

"Fine then. Go be friends with Kit," Fran said.

"Maybe I will," Jen said. And maybe she would.

Kit was nice. She brought out the best in Jen. Kit would be the right kind of friend for Jen.

"Hey Kit," Jen called, "Want to stop for a cold drink after practice?"

Kit smiled. "I'd love to," she said.